LAST TO FINIS

MATH CLASS

A STORY ABOUT LEARNING DIFFERENTLY

WORDS BY
BARBARA ESHAM

PICTURES BY
MIKE AND CARL GORDON

sourcebooks eXplore

I always thought that math was going to be my thing.

My dad is an engineer, and he always says that math is the key to success.

It is just my luck that the door to success is locked with the "math" keys.

SUCCESS
MATH

I'm Max Leonhard, and I'm a third grader at Perryville Elementary School.

This year has been a bit tough for me because it's the first time that I ever felt I was completely terrible at something...

and that doesn't feel so good.

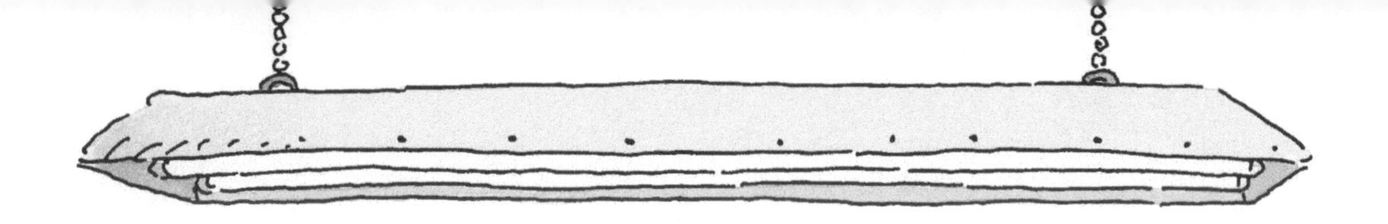

The problem started when Mrs. Topel, our teacher, started using the timer to test us on our multiplication facts.

If I take my time, I can get every one of my math facts without any problem at all!

The problem comes when I have to finish them in record time—like a sprinter running toward the finish line, hoping to break the world record.

The timer works just fine for some kids, like David Peterson. He likes to be the first to finish everything!

It doesn't work for me.

As soon as Mrs. Topel starts the timer,
my heart begins to pound,
my hands begin to sweat,
and then the worst thing happens...

MY MIND FREEZES.

It happened again today.

One by one, my classmates finished their math facts. I knew the answers last night when I did my practice test, but they disappeared today!

All I could think about was that terrible timer ticking that terrible tick-tick-tick!

What happened?

Are math facts erased from my mind while I sleep?

Why does 2x3 suddenly look like an alien message that only scientists can decipher?

"TIME IS UP," Mrs. Topel announced.

I was the last one to hand in my paper and I still had twenty problems to go.

Just when I thought things couldn't get any worse, David Peterson whispered, "Max, Max, last in math."

In the lunch room after math class, during physical education and art, David continued to tease me.

He would not stop.

Does embarrassing me make David Peterson feel important for some reason?

The chanting started up again during recess, as I knew it would. The chanting was so loud that even the preschool class could hear it.

They thought it was okay to chant along.

"MAX, MAX, LAST IN MATH!"

After school, I went straight home to do my homework, and the day got even worse. I couldn't find my math folder.

I emptied my backpack to search for it,
which wasn't such a bad idea...
I needed to get rid of a few things.

"Mom, I can't find my math folder," I admitted.
It was a little embarrassing.

"Max, you are going to have to be more responsible with your school work, especially your math materials," she replied.

Sometimes I get the feeling that my mom and dad are disappointed in me.

I know they love me, but I want them to be proud of me too.

Maybe I'm just disappointed in myself.

Timed math facts have ruined everything!

"Max, Mrs. Topel and Mr. Singleton have asked us to attend a meeting. They want to discuss your math performance. I'm sure that everything will be just fine.

"Remember, Max, your dad and I are proud of your hard work. You may just need to work a little harder," my mom said with a smile.

My parents had been encouraging about the conference, but I was nervous when it was time to meet a few days later.

I expected Mrs. Topel and Mr. Singleton to tell my parents that I was the worst math student they'd ever taught at Perryville Elementary.

The fateful day arrived.

“Mr. and Mrs. Leonhard, thank you for taking the time to meet with us today,” Mr. Singleton said with a serious voice.

“About two weeks ago, I found Max’s math folder in the hallway. I didn’t return it because I was very surprised by the math exercises Max has been working on,” he added.

"We thought it was important that we discuss Max's math ability with you," Mrs. Topel said.

Math ability? I thought. *What math ability?*

I'm always the last to finish my math facts. I guess it's the lack of ability we'll be discussing. I knew this conference wouldn't be good...

"How long has Max been practicing algebra?" Mr. Singleton asked.

"Algebra? There must be a mistake," my dad said. "Max is only in third grade." My mom looked confused. "Max, what is Mr. Singleton talking about?"

"Algebra is something I do for fun.
It's like a puzzle.

"I finished my older brother Eric's pre-algebra book last year, so sometimes I borrow his algebra book—if he isn't using it of course," I said.

"All this time, we've been concerned about Max's math performance. He has struggled with memorizing multiplication facts all year," my dad said.

"Max is the type of math student who understands how numbers work together. He may not be the type of student who learns by memorization. Some people are great at memorizing all sorts of information, while others are great at understanding information. If I could choose between the two, I would rather have students understand mathematics," Mr. Singleton said.

"Does this mean that Max will move ahead to algebra?" my dad asked.

"We will need to be sure that Max has a complete understanding of the math concepts leading up to algebra. Max will spend some of his time with the algebra class so he can build on what he has mastered," said Mr. Singleton.

"I would also like him to join our math team. He would make an excellent addition."

"Me? On the math team?
That is the strangest thing I have ever heard!" I said.

"Not really, Max. You seem to be an algebra wiz.
Let's give it a try," my dad added, quite proudly.

"Well, maybe I'll give it a try," I said.
"But only under one condition..."

"No timer!"

A NOTE TO CARING ADULTS

FROM DR. EDWARD HALLOWELL

New York Times national bestseller, former Harvard Medical School instructor, and current director of the Hallowell Center for Cognitive and Emotional Health

Fear is the great disabler. Fear is what keeps children from realizing their potential. It needs to be replaced with a feeling of I-know-I-can-make-progress-if-I-keep-trying-and-boy-do-I-ever-want-to-do-that!

One of the great goals of parents, teachers, and coaches should be to find areas in which a child might experience mastery, then make it possible for the child to feel this potent sensation. The feeling of mastery transforms a child from a reluctant, fearful learner into a self-motivated player. The mistake that parents, teachers, and coaches often make is that they demand mastery rather than lead children to it by helping them overcome the fear of failure. The best parents are great teachers. My definition of a great teacher is a person who can lead another person to mastery.

ARE YOU AN EVERYDAY GENIUS TOO?

Everyday geniuses are **creative,** STRONG, **thoughtful,**
and sometimes learn a little differently from others.
And that's what makes them so special!

In *Last to Finish in Math Class*, Max is always the last student to finish his timed math tests. Some of the kids tease him about it and he feels like he's not very smart.

Have you ever felt like you weren't very good at something? Has anyone ever teased you about not being as good as someone else?

What happened?

Max's teacher realized that he was actually very good at math, but just not good at memorizing facts. Sometimes we have to find what we are good at and then build from there because the bad things seem to overshadow everything else.

Here are a few other things you can do:

- Ask your teacher or another caring adult for help. Other people may have some advice on how to get better. But they can't help you if they don't know what's going on.
- Find the things you're good at. Can you use those good things to help you in the areas that you're struggling? If you're really good at basketball but you are struggling in math, can you turn your math problems into basketball problems?
- Change the view. If you're struggling with something, try to do that same thing in a new setting. You might discover that it's something in your environment that is stressing you out or creating a distraction. Try doing your homework in a different room or sitting in a different chair and see how it feels!

In this story, Max struggled with timed tests but he was really good in advanced math. Not everyone who struggles in a subject is a hidden genius in that same subject. But it is true that we all learn a little differently and need help in different ways. The most important thing to remember is that none of us is hopeless or a disappointment. We are all good in some things and not so in others. That's what makes us all special!

Remember, everyday geniuses are creative, strong, thoughtful, and sometimes learn a little differently from others. It's never a bad thing to be different—embracing and learning from our differences is what makes the world a better place!

ABOUT THE AUTHOR

Author Barbara Esham was one of those kids who couldn't resist performing a pressure test on a pudding cup. She has always been a "free association" thinker, finding life far more interesting while in a state of abstract thought. Barbara lives on the East Coast with her three daughters. Together, in Piagetian fashion, they have explored the ideas and theories behind the definitions of intelligence, creativity, learning, and success. Barb researches and writes from her home office in the spare time available between car pools, homework, and bedtime.

ABOUT THE ILLUSTRATORS

Cartooning has brought Mike Gordon acclaim in worldwide competitions, adding to his international reputation as a top humorous illustrator. Since 1993 he has continued his successful career based in California, gaining a nomination in the prestigious National Cartoonist Society Awards. Mike is the renowned illustrator for the wildly popular book series beginning with *Do Princesses Wear Hiking Boots?* Mike collaborates with his son Carl Gordon from across the world. They have been a team since 1999. Mike creates the line illustrations, and the color is applied by Carl using a graphics tablet and computer. Carl has a degree in graphic art and currently lives in Cape Town, South Africa, with his wife and kids.

Illustrations by Mike and Carl Gordon
Cover design by Travis Hasenour

The story text was set in OpenDyslexic, a font specifically designed for readability with dyslexia.
The back matter was set in Adobe Garamond Pro.

Published by Sourcebooks eXplore, an imprint of Sourcebooks Kids
P.O. Box 4410, Naperville, Illinois 60567-4410
(630) 961-3900
sourcebookskids.com

Originally published as *Last to Finish: A Story About the Smartest Boy in Math Class* in 2008 in the United States of America by Mainstream Connections Publishing. This edition issued based on the hardcover edition published in 2018 in the United States of America by Sourcebooks Kids.
Cataloging-in-Publication Data is on file with the Library of Congress.

Source of Production: Lightning Source, Inc., La Vergne, TN, USA
Date of Production: May 2024
Run Number: 5040833

Printed and bound in the United States of America.
LSI 10 9 8 7 6 5 4 3 2 1

Printed in the USA
CPSIA information can be obtained
at www.ICGtesting.com
CBHW041043220424
7194CB00001B/4

9 781728 289434